Fairy Realm

BOOK 10

The Rainbow Wand

ALSO BY EMILY RODDA

FAIRY REALM

ROWAN OF RIN

Fairy Realm

The Rainbow Wand

BOOK 10

EMILY RODDA

ILLUSTRATIONS BY RAOUL VITALE

■ HARPERCOLLINS *PUBLISHERS*

The Rainbow Wand

Text copyright © 2006 by Emily Rodda

Illustrations copyright © 2006 by Raoul Vitale

www.harperchildrens.com

Library of Congress Cataloging-in-Publication Data

Rodda, Emily.

The rainbow wand / Emily Rodda ; illustrations by Raoul Vitale.— 1st
ed.

p.   cm. — (Fairy realm ; bk. 10)

Summary: When a little girl from the human world becomes lost in the
magical Realm, Jessie's only hope of finding her is the wand of a brilliant
but reclusive magician, and if she succeeds she must still face Mrs.
Tweedie, who is up to no good.

ISBN-10: 0-06-077768-0 (trade bdg.)

ISBN-13: 978-0-06-077768-5 (trade bdg.)

ISBN-10: 0-06-077769-9 (lib. bdg.)

ISBN-13: 978-0-06-077769-2 (lib. bdg.)

[1. Lost children — Fiction. 2. Magic — Fiction. 3. Fairies — Fiction.]
I. Vitale, Raoul, ill. II. Title. III. Series: Rodda, Emily. Fairy realm ; bk. 10.
PZ7.R5996Rai 2006   2006000341
[Fic] — dc22   CIP
                                                                              AC

Typography by Karin Paprocki

2 3 4 5 6 7 8 9 10

❖

First Edition

CONTENTS

Fairy Realm

Book 10

The Rainbow Wand

sticky-beak

The flower fairies whirled around Jessie in a fluttering blur of pink, blue, green, purple, yellow, and white. Their bright wings brushed Jessie's cheeks. Their tiny fingers tangled in her golden red hair. Their voices rang in her ears like crystal bells.

"Don't go, Jessie! Queen Helena is in the west, and we've got no one to dance with us. Stay in the Realm and dance with us, Jessie! Oh, please, please, please!"

"Rose! Bluebell! Violet! Daffodil! Daisy! Stop this!" Jessie laughed. "I have to go back to my

1

own world now. It's Saturday, and Mum's home. She'll be wondering where I am. I'll dance with you next time I visit, I promise."

"But that won't be for a long time!" cried Daisy. "That's what you said to Patrice the palace housekeeper, and Giff the elf, and Maybelle the little white horse."

"You said you had to stay away from the Realm—because of a nasty old sticky-beak!" added Bluebell.

"Oh, you naughty fairies!" Jessie exclaimed. "You were hiding! You were listening!"

Bluebell and Violet hung their heads, but Daffodil, Daisy, and Rose giggled.

"Yes," said Daffodil, smoothing her yellow skirts. "We were hiding in the Ding Dong tree and we heard. What's a sticky-beak, Jessie? What, what, what?"

"Someone who pokes her nose into other people's business!" said Jessie, trying hard to sound stern. She faced the shadowy archway that marked the border of the Realm. "Open!" she called.

She closed her eyes as shadows surrounded

her. Her skin prickled as the familiar cool, tingling breeze swept her away.

Then, suddenly, everything grew still again. She could hear birds singing. The tangy scent of rosemary filled the air.

Jessie opened her eyes. She was standing on a small square of smooth green grass. The grass was edged with rosemary bushes and surrounded by a high, clipped hedge. She was back in the place she called the secret garden. She was home.

Quickly she checked to see that the door in the hedge was still shut and that the spade she'd wedged against the old latch was still firmly in place. She breathed a sigh of relief when she saw that everything was just as she'd left it.

No one had tried to enter the secret garden while she was away. Now all she had to do was get back to the house without—

"Surprise!" squealed five tiny voices. And there were the flower fairies, dancing in the air in front of her, their faces filled with glee.

"We tricked you, Jessie!" shrieked Daffodil. "We came with you!"

"Now you can dance with us *here*!" squeaked Rose, dipping and twirling so that her frilly pink skirts billowed out around her and the tails of her green sash flew.

"No, I can't!" said Jessie, hiding a smile. "I have to go up to the house. Mum will be—"

Suddenly anxious, Jessie ran to the door in the hedge, opened it cautiously, and peered out. The Blue Moon garden was deserted except for the birds chattering in the trees. Her mother, Rosemary, was nowhere to be seen, and for once there was no sign of Louise Tweedie, their nosy next-door neighbor, either.

Jessie breathed a sigh of relief. It had been a good idea to visit the Realm today—the day when the inside of Mrs. Tweedie's house was going to be painted. She'd hoped that Mrs. Tweedie would be too busy fussing around the painters to be bothered about Blue Moon, and it looked as if she'd been right. Still . . .

She turned back to the fairies. "You should go back to the Realm now," she said. "Someone might see you."

Shy little Violet looked worried, but Daisy grinned. "No one sees us," she boasted, swinging on a stem of rosemary. "If they do, they think we're flutterbyes."

"Flutterbyes, flutterbyes!" Daffodil giggled, opening and closing her yellow wings.

"They might think you're butterflies at first," Jessie argued. "But what if they look more closely? What if—?"

"Your grandmother, our true Queen, likes it when we come to her garden to play, Jessie," Bluebell said seriously. "And lately she has been making a new game—"

"I see one!" shrieked Rose. She darted under a rosemary bush, then fluttered back out onto the grass clutching something that looked like a tiny green-and-white-striped pillow.

"Sweetie-pies!"

With squeals of excitement, the other fairies began flying around, searching for more hidden treats.

"Quickly, quickly!" squeaked Daffodil. "Find them all before the rainbow fairies come and find them first! Emerald said that they found nine sweetie-pies yesterday. *Nine!* Pink-striped, green-striped, purple-striped . . ."

Jessie knew that there was no way she was going to make the fairies leave now. Frowning slightly, she closed the door in the hedge behind her and began walking up toward the house. For the first time in her life, she felt annoyed with her beloved grandmother.

Why has Granny put treats for the fairies in the secret garden? she thought crossly. Doesn't she realize that it's risky to encourage them to come here too often just now?

No, she doesn't! Jessie stopped suddenly as the thought struck her.

Granny had lived at Blue Moon for over fifty years, ever since she had left her life as a princess of the Realm to marry Robert Belairs, the human man she loved. For all that time the Blue Moon garden had been safe for any fairy, pixie, or other magical creature who had cared to visit.

But Granny had been away for two whole weeks, because the long-awaited exhibition of

Robert Belairs's fairy paintings had begun at the National Gallery. The real trouble hadn't started till after she left.

Granny didn't know just how much of a pest Mrs. Tweedie had become. She didn't know that the woman was not only prying in the house, but had started making endless, feeble excuses for prowling around the Blue Moon garden.

Oh, I wish Mrs. Tweedie had never come here! Jessie thought angrily as she started hurrying toward the house again. Why did the Bins family have to rent their house to *her*?

The Bins family had been awful neighbors, but at least they'd kept away from Blue Moon. In fact, most of the time they'd tried to pretend that the house, and its unusual owner, just didn't exist. Until that last, terrible day when they'd found out just how unusual Jessie's grandmother was.

Luckily, no one had believed their terrified babblings of fairy queens and unicorns. Everyone thought they'd lost their minds. After that, they'd fled to the city, and no one in the mountains had seen them since.

Jessie had been very happy to see them go. It had never occurred to her that the person who came to live in the house after them might be even worse.

Jessie trudged on, glaring through the gaps in the trees at the house next door. It wouldn't have surprised her to see a red-tipped nose poking over the fence or a pair of sharp eyes peering from one of the windows.

"Poor Louise." Jessie's mother had laughed when Jessie had complained about Mrs. Tweedie. "She's just lonely. What does it matter if she wanders around in here? It's not as if we have anything to hide."

But we do, Mum, Jessie had thought desperately. You just don't know it. And for the millionth time, she'd wished her mother *did* know about the Realm, and the secret Door at the bottom of the Blue Moon garden.

"There are Doors to the Realm all over the world, Jessie," her grandmother had told her. "But only people who believe in magic can find them. That's what keeps the Doors safe. Everyone has to discover the Realm for himself or herself. As you did, when you first came to live here—and as my Robert did long ago."

But Rosemary had spent her childhood at Blue Moon. How could it be that she'd never seen a fairy, pixie, or elf in all that time?

She probably *did* see them, actually, Jessie thought as she reached the back door and pulled it open. She just didn't realize what they were. Mum doesn't believe in fairies—Granny said she never did, even when she was little. She didn't expect to see fairies and so she didn't. If she caught sight of them out of the corner of her eye, she thought they were butterflies, or shadows, or leaves blowing in the wind.

And Rosemary had never suspected as she watched her father painting the fairyland pictures that had made him famous that he was painting things he'd really seen. Like everyone else, she just thought he had a wonderful imagination.

Jessie went into the warm kitchen and pulled off her jacket. She was just about to call her mother when she heard the sound of voices drifting from the living room. She groaned silently. So Mrs. Tweedie hadn't been able to do without her daily visit after all!

She thought of going outside again, then decided to tiptoe to her room instead. She crept into the hallway, trying not to make the old boards creak.

"It was very good of you to take the trouble to come," Jessie heard her mother say from the living room.

"It was no trouble," a cool voice answered. "I've been wanting to talk to you about this for a while. Then I heard that the Open Day was tomorrow, so naturally . . ."

Jessie froze. That wasn't Mrs. Tweedie's voice. It belonged to the person who was the second biggest problem in her life: her schoolteacher, Ms. Stone.

unwelcome guests

Why is old Stoneface here? Jessie thought in panic. I haven't done anything to annoy her lately. Well, except reading that book about pixies in reading time on Friday. But L. T. Bowers is a well-known writer, and I did get the book out of the library. And I haven't written any fairy stories for ages, or talked about fairy things, or—

"I'll think carefully about what you've said, Lyn," said Rosemary. "Of course, I'm delighted that you think Jessie's so talented. But—"

"Naturally it's a difficult decision for you," Ms Stone broke in smoothly. "But you have Jessica

13

future to think about. A city school like March-banks that specializes in guiding talented students is just what she needs."

Jessie's stomach turned over. She pressed her hand to her mouth, listening intently.

"Houses and flats are expensive in the city, I know," she heard Ms. Stone say. "Still, sacrifices have to be made if—"

"Actually, I didn't sell our city house when we came here," Rosemary said quietly. "It's rented, at the moment. I haven't been able to make up my mind to sell, just in case. . . . But, the thing is, Lyn, Jessie loves living here, at Blue Moon. She's very close to her grandmother, and—"

"If you'll forgive me for saying so, Rosemary, I think that's half the trouble," Ms. Stone inter-upted. "Because you go out to work, Jessica nds a lot of time alone with Mrs. Belairs. Isn't ?"

yes," said Rosemary, sounding a bit "But—"

ver met Mrs. Belairs," Ms. Stone 's fascination with old-fashioned

14

fairy stories and fantasy clearly shows her grand-mother's influence. Frankly, it's the worst influence in the world for her. She's reading all sorts of rubbish—fiction that pretends to be fact. And she's not developing her writing talent as she should."

Jessie's face was burning. She wanted to run in there shouting to her mother not to listen, not to believe a word Ms. Stone was saying. But then she'd have to admit she'd been lurking in the hall-way listening.

"Well, I'll leave you to think about it," said Ms. Stone. "But do try to get to the Marchbanks Open Day tomorrow. I'm sure you'll be very impressed."

There was the sound of movement, as though she was rising to her feet. Jessie darted back to the kitchen, out of sight.

"Thank you again, Lyn," she heard her mother say as the front door opened. "You're very good to take such an interest in Jessie."

"She reminds me of myself as a child," said Ms. Stone abruptly. "Intelligent but dreamy, with no control over her imagination. Her mind is cluttered

15

with useless fancies — as mine was, for a long, long time."

Jessie listened, fascinated. She found it hard to imagine cool, confident Ms. Stone being a child, let alone a dreamy one. In the classroom, Ms. Stone was interested in nothing but facts, facts, facts.

"My foster parents were good people, but they didn't understand me at all," Ms. Stone said. "For a while they tried to make me focus on practical things. Then they just gave up and let me dream my childhood away."

"I suppose they thought it was best not to push you," said Rosemary.

"I suppose so," Ms. Stone agreed coolly. "But the result was that I grew up feeling a stranger in the real world. I couldn't tell fact from fantasy, and I couldn't cope with real-life problems. My foster parents died when I was in my teens, and after that, life became very hard for me. I was difficult and lonely. I had trouble making friends. I survived, but it wasn't easy."

Her voice hardened. "As a teacher, I'm determined not to let any child in my care go through what I did if I can prevent it. That's why I refuse to allow fantasy in my classroom. And that's why I'm here today."

"I understand," Rosemary said. Her voice was serious and rather sad.

"A school like Marchbanks would have been the best thing that had ever happened to me," Ms. Stone said flatly. "Just as, in my opinion, it would be the best thing for Jessica."

Jessie groped her way to the back door and silently let herself out. She sat on the step taking great gulps of fresh, cool air, trying to calm down.

Mum won't take me away to some special school just because Ms. Stone says so, she told herself. Mum knows that I'm not like Ms. Stone was. *I* have friends. *I* can handle real-life problems.

But Ms. Stone had been so earnest, and so convincing! And her mother had sounded very serious and sad, as if she'd begun to think Ms. Stone might be right.

Jessie heard the sound of a car starting up at the front of the house. Ms. Stone was leaving.

Jessie got to her feet and went back into the house, shutting the door loudly behind her.

"Jessie, is that you?" she heard her mother call.

"Yes," Jessie called back.

Rosemary came into the kitchen. Without a word, she crossed the room and put her arms around Jessie, hugging her tightly.

"Is something wrong, Mum?" asked Jessie. She held her breath, waiting for Rosemary to tell her about Ms. Stone's visit.

"Of course not," said Rosemary, standing back and forcing a smile. "I was just thinking—how grown-up you're getting. I'll make us some lunch. What do you feel like?"

She went to the refrigerator and looked inside. "It might be better for you to go to Sal's for the day tomorrow instead of coming with me to the airport to pick up Granny," she said, without turning around. "I've decided to leave here very early. There are a few things I'd like to do before I go to the airport."

Like go to the Marchbanks Open Day, Jessie thought dismally. Oh, Mum!

There was a light tap on the back door. "Yoo-hoo, it's only me!" called Mrs. Tweedie, sounding far less chirpy than usual.

Rosemary sighed and turned away from the fridge. "Come in, Louise," she called back.

Mrs. Tweedie tottered into the kitchen, a wad of tissues held to her nose and tears streaming from her puffy, red-rimmed eyes. "It's the fumes from the new paint," she said snuffling, before anyone could ask her what was wrong. "I'm always sensitive to things like that. But I didn't like to object when Mr. Bins said the house had to be painted."

"Oh, what a nuisance for you, Louise," said Rosemary, looking concerned.

Mrs. Tweedie sank into a chair and hunched there, sniffing dolefully. Her spiky hair was ruffled. She looked like a bedraggled hen.

She smells like one, too, Jessie thought, wrinkling her nose. Or she smells of something. She's rubbed some stuff on her chest to unblock her nose, I suppose.

"I don't know what I'm going to do," Mrs.

19

Tweedie moaned, putting her head in her hands. "I can't stay in that house, but I've got nowhere else to go."

Jessie glanced urgently at her mother. Don't ask her here, she begged silently. Don't ask her. . . .

"I rang Mr. Bins, but he just said I should move into a motel for a couple of days." Mrs. Tweedie sniffed. "He doesn't seem to understand that I can't possibly afford—"

"Louise, don't be silly," said Rosemary, frowning at Jessie, who was mouthing "No! No!" and shaking her head. "You can stay here. We've got a spare room."

Mrs. Tweedie lifted her head, and Jessie was sure she saw a spark of triumph in the watery, red-rimmed eyes.

"Oh, that would be wonderful!" Mrs. Tweedie gasped. Then she clasped her hands anxiously. "But your mother gets home tomorrow afternoon, doesn't she, Rosemary? And you and Jessie are going down to pick her up? You'll all be very tired when you get home. You won't want a stranger—"

"It won't be any trouble at all, Louise," Rosemary

broke in firmly. "Mum will be pleased to see you. I'm just sorry you'll have to spend the day on your own."

Jessie took a deep breath. "Mum," she said, "if Mrs. Tweedie is going to be here, then I can stay here, too, can't I? I mean, I don't need to go to Sal's at all."

Rosemary's eyes widened. She couldn't understand why Jessie would want to spend the day with Mrs. Tweedie. And Jessie *didn't* want to, not at all. But she wanted to leave Mrs. Tweedie alone at Blue Moon even less.

"Jessie's not going with me," Rosemary explained to Mrs. Tweedie, who was also looking surprised. "She was going to spend the day with a friend. But—"

"Oh, you mustn't change your plans for *me*, Jessie," Mrs. Tweedie exclaimed. "That really *would* upset me."

"It's okay," Jessie said sweetly. "I've—I've got lots of homework to do, anyway. I'd really rather stay home."

A trace of annoyance crossed Mrs. Tweedie's

face. It disappeared instantly, but Jessie had seen it.

Got you! she thought with grim satisfaction. You thought your chance had come, didn't you? You thought you'd have a whole day to prowl around Blue Moon and sticky-beak everywhere with no one to see what you were doing. Well, too bad. I'm staying.

suspicion

In ten minutes, Mrs. Tweedie had moved into the small spare bedroom across the hall from Jessie's room. Rosemary found some clean sheets while Jessie carried in Mrs. Tweedie's neat little overnight bag, which was surprisingly heavy. Mrs. Tweedie thanked them over and over again, then insisted they leave her to settle in. Gratefully, Jessie and Rosemary escaped to the kitchen. It was such a relief to get away from her constant talking.

"Her bag was already packed, Mum," Jessie whispered as her mother began chopping onions to make soup for dinner. "She *knew* you'd ask her to stay."

"Of course she did," Rosemary whispered back, blinking as the onion began to make her eyes water. "But that doesn't make any difference. You could see for yourself what the paint fumes had done to her. The poor thing was—"

"Oh!" Jessie squealed.

Rosemary jumped in shock, nearly dropping the knife. "Jessie, I almost cut myself!" she exclaimed. "What's the matter with you?"

"Onion!" Jessie breathed. "That's what Mrs. Tweedie smelled of when she came in: raw onion! Mum, she doesn't have an allergy at all! She used onion to make her eyes water and go red!"

Rosemary sighed and turned back to the chopping board. "Jessie, you're letting your imagination run away with you," she said. "You don't like Mrs. Tweedie, but that's no excuse for being mean. The poor woman is here because she didn't have anywhere else to go."

"Well, if she's so poor, why did she rent the Bins's house?" Jessie snapped back. "Why didn't she rent something smaller?"

"She probably got a special deal," Rosemary said, wiping her eyes on her sleeve. "She knows the Bins family quite well, I think. They rented the apartment next door to hers for a while, when they first went back to the city."

Jessie's jaw dropped. "Mrs. Tweedie lived next door to the *Bins*?" She gasped. "Does Granny know that?"

"Well, I don't suppose she does," Rosemary said. "I'd more or less forgotten about it myself till now. Louise let it slip to me one day. I don't think she meant to because she got very flustered and started rattling on about something else."

She grinned. "She was probably embarrassed. She must know we weren't friendly with the Bins family. You can imagine what they said to her about us. Jess, could you go out and get me some parsley, please?"

Jessie almost ran to the back door, escaping from the house with relief. The discovery that Mrs. Tweedie actually knew the Bins family had left her breathless.

What *had* the Bins told Mrs. Tweedie? What if they'd told her about the strange things they'd seen and heard at Blue Moon? And what if Mrs. Tweedie hadn't thought they were crazy? What if she'd believed them?

That would explain a lot. It would explain why, from the very beginning, Mrs. Tweedie had been so interested in Blue Moon—and why she was always making excuses to wander around the garden. Poking her sharp, little nose into every hidden corner, peering about with those bright, darting eyes . . .

Jessie knelt down and clumsily picked a small bunch of parsley from the patch near the back door. Her fingers felt stiff. Her heart was thudding wildly. She heard a small, enquiring trill and looked up. Flynn, Granny's big orange cat, was sitting on the grass nearby, watching her.

"I think Mrs. Tweedie knows about the Realm, Flynn," Jessie whispered. "Or she suspects something, anyway. And now she's actually staying in the house! Granny will be home tomorrow night, and she'll know what to do. But until then we mustn't let Mrs. Tweedie out of our sight. Not for a minute."

"Jessie!"

Jessie looked quickly around. Her mother was standing at the back door with her hands on her hips. "Jessie, I'm waiting for that parsley!" Rosemary exclaimed. "What are you doing crouched there, talking to yourself?"

"Oh, sorry!" gabbled Jessie, scrambling to her feet. "But I wasn't talking to myself. I was talking to Flynn."

"Oh, really?" said Rosemary dryly. "You're getting as bad as your grandmother." She turned and went back into the house.

Jessie followed miserably. Her worry about Mrs. Tweedie had made her forget Ms. Stone's visit for a while. Now the memory of it returned in full force.

Oh, why had she said she'd been talking to Flynn? It seemed that everything she did gave her mother even more reason to think that the sooner she was away from Granny, the better.

❉ ❉ ❉

Rosemary left early the next morning. Before she went, she urged Jessie to go to Sal's for the day as planned. "You and Sal are still good friends, aren't you?" she asked, a little anxiously.

"Of course we are!" said Jessie, the memory of Ms. Stone's remarks about friends very clear in her mind. "I just don't want to leave Mrs. Tweedie here on her own."

Rosemary took a breath to say something, then changed her mind and shook her head helplessly instead.

Jessie waved until the car was out of sight. Then, sick at heart, she returned to the kitchen. It didn't improve her mood to find Mrs. Tweedie, in a smart cherry red dressing gown and matching slippers, standing at the kitchen bench, making coffee.

Flynn was crouched by the door, watching Mrs. Tweedie with slitted eyes. He looked half asleep, but Jessie knew he was fully alert, keeping his part of their bargain.

"Good morning, dear," Mrs. Tweedie chirped, replacing the lid on a tin of strong-smelling coffee she'd obviously brought from home.

"Are you feeling better today, Mrs. Tweedie?" Jessie asked.

"Oh, yes," Mrs. Tweedie said brightly. "Now that I'm away from that awful paint I'm feeling almost as good as new."

In fact, she looked even better than new, Jessie thought. The red dressing gown suited her much better than the dowdy, old-lady clothes she usually wore. Her eyes were clear and sparkling. Even her movements as she poured her coffee and sat down at the table were firmer and less fussy than usual. It was as if she'd become years younger overnight.

"I'd be *quite* all right on my own today, you know," said Mrs. Tweedie, looking up at Jessie over the rim of her coffee cup. "Are you sure you don't want to go to Sal's after all?"

"Oh, no," Jessie answered lightly. "I'm fine here, really."

Again she saw a flash of anger in the bright bird's eyes. Then the eyes dropped, and for a few minutes Mrs. Tweedie sat in silence, drinking her coffee thoughtfully.

This is like a game of chess, Jessie said to herself. What's her next move going to be?

The next move was unexpected. Mrs. Tweedie stood up, put her coffee cup in the sink, and announced that she was going to have a nice, quiet day. Then she simply went to her room and shut the door behind her.

Jessie spent the next few hours in her own room, trying to read her library book, but finding it very hard to concentrate. The book had some fuzzy-looking black-and-white pictures that showed what were supposed to be pixies, photographed in secret. The pixies could have been anything from toadstools to cardboard cutouts, but L. T. Bowers seemed to have no doubt that they were real.

Restlessly, Jessie turned to the front of the book and read the titles of the other books L. T. Bowers had written: *Haunted Houses of the World* . . . *Bigfoot: Fact or Fable?* . . . *The Loch Ness Monster* . . .

Her attention wandered. Her door was wide open, and the spare room was right across the hall. She'd know at once if Mrs. Tweedie came out. But still she found herself glancing up over and over again.

Maybe I'm being as silly as Mum thinks I am, she thought. Maybe I'm giving myself a miserable, boring Sunday all for nothing. But she turned back to her place and sat stubbornly staring at *Pixies on the Moor*, reading the same sentences over and over again, while the morning slipped away.

At midday, the doorbell rang, making her jump. The spare room door snapped open and Mrs. Tweedie appeared, wearing slim black trousers, a white silk shirt, and a red jacket. "I'll get it," she chirped, flashing a smile at Jessie. She shut the door behind her and strode quickly away.

Jessie heard her open the front door. She heard the murmur of voices, among them the high, piping voice of a young child. At the same moment, a draft swept down the hallway. The spare room door clicked and swung open, giving Jessie a clear view of Mrs. Tweedie's belongings arranged neatly on the old desk that stood beside the bed.

A laptop computer, its screen dark. A very

expensive-looking camera. A video camera. A mobile phone.

Jessie's eyes widened. She didn't know exactly how much all these things cost, but she did know that they weren't the possessions of someone who was as short of money as Mrs. Tweedie claimed to be.

Neither is that red dressing gown, she thought suddenly. Or even the coffee. Mrs. Tweedie isn't poor! She just pretends she is.

Just like she pretends she's just a fussy, harmless old duck, a voice in her mind added, when really she's nothing of the kind.

A tingling feeling ran down Jessie's spine.

CHAPTER FOUR

Tasha

The front door closed, but Mrs. Tweedie was still talking. Realizing that someone had come in, Jessie put her book down and hurried out of her room.

At the kitchen door she met Mrs. Tweedie and a wide-eyed little girl of about four. The girl was wearing pink overalls, a pink-and-white-striped top, and a pair of silver fairy wings. A gauzy butterfly was clipped to her short, black curls. She was clutching a battered blue rabbit.

"Ah, there you are, Jessie," said Mrs. Tweedie, in a falsely sweet voice. "This is my little friend

Tasha. Tasha and Bunny have come to visit me, while their mummy goes to work. Isn't that lovely?"

"Oh—yes," Jessie stammered. Tasha put her finger in her mouth and crushed the blue rabbit more tightly to her chest.

"Do you know, yesterday I'd quite forgotten that Tasha was coming today?" Mrs. Tweedie went on, still in that awful, fake voice. "Then, this morning I remembered. So I rang Tasha's mummy and told her that my house is full of nasty paint smells, so Tasha could visit me here, instead."

Tasha took her finger out of her mouth. "In the fairy house," she said.

"That's right!" said Mrs. Tweedie, glancing quickly at Jessie. "Now, Tasha, would you like an ice cream? You like ice cream, don't you?"

"Yes!" said Tasha, her face breaking into a smile. "With chockie on."

"You ask Jessie if she'll go to the shops and buy us all a chocolate-coated ice cream, then," said Mrs. Tweedie. "Ask her very, very nicely. Say, '*Please*, Jessie!'"

"*Please*, Jessie!" Tasha repeated, her face glowing.

"Pretty please," cooed Mrs. Tweedie, handing Jessie some money.

Jessie didn't want to go anywhere, but she knew she had no choice. She just couldn't say no to the little girl who was looking up at her so trustingly.

And Mrs. Tweedie knows it, too, she thought angrily as she left the house and hurried up the street. She's got rid of me at last.

She found that she was almost running, and forced herself to slow down. Don't be stupid, she told herself sternly. You'll be away only half an hour. Anyway, Mrs. Tweedie won't be able to do much spying with a four year old trailing around after her, watching everything she does. She'd be too scared of Tasha talking about it to me afterward.

Still, she fretted as she made her long way to the shops, waited to be served, and jogged home again. She knew she wouldn't be happy until she had Mrs. Tweedie safely under her eye again.

❊ ❊ ❊

The house was quiet when Jessie got home. Even Flynn was nowhere to be seen.

"Hello!" Jessie called, thrusting the melting ice creams into the freezer. "Mrs. Tweedie? Tasha?"

Then she saw the note on the kitchen table. The writing was Mrs. Tweedie's, but it was scrawled, as though it had been written in a rush.

Jessie —
Tasha is missing. I only turned my back for a minute, and she was gone. She's nowhere in the house or garden. Might have tried to walk home. I'm going out to look for her.
Mrs. T.

Jessie stared at the note, a hot tide of anger washing over her. Only turned your back for a minute, did you? she thought furiously. Oh, sure! I'll bet you nipped off to sticky-beak in Grandpa's studio as soon as I'd gone and left Tasha by herself. How could you be so stupid?

The anger was quickly replaced by fear, as she thought of a four year old walking the streets alone. Did Tasha even *know* her way home from Blue Moon? What if she'd wandered into the woods at the end of the street? How long had she been missing? Ten minutes? Twenty?

Flynn! she thought suddenly. Where's Flynn? He might know where Tasha is.

She bolted through the back door, almost colliding with a bald man in paint-smeared white overalls who was standing on the back step, with his hand raised to knock.

"Oh, sorry, love," the man said. "Mrs. Tweedie there?"

"Have you seen a little dark-haired girl anywhere?" Jessie gasped. "A four-year-old girl? Carrying a blue rabbit? Wearing a pink—"

"Nope," the man said. "Haven't seen her, sorry. Look, I need a word with Mrs. Tweedie."

"She's not here," said Jessie. "She's gone to—"

"Strike me lucky," the man said, his forehead wrinkling all the way up to his bald scalp. "She lays it on us to work this weekend, says it's *got* to be this weekend—though it beats me why it's so urgent when the old paint's still good as new and

41

she's not even changing the color. Then she goes off and leaves us flat!"

He turned away. "You just tell her we're painting the bedroom cupboards same as the doors, then, will you love?" he said. "Double pay or no double pay, we can't hang around waiting. Got to start another job Monday."

He slouched off, shaking his head and muttering to himself. Jessie stared after him in confusion. He'd talked as if Mrs. Tweedie had organized the painting of the house herself, but the painting was all Mr. Bins's doing.

Or *was* it? They only had Mrs. Tweedie's word for it. And the more Jessie thought about what the painter had said, the more she doubted that Mrs. Tweedie had been telling the truth. There was no way Mr. Bins would spend money on having his house painted if it didn't need it. And there was no way he'd pay double to get the job done on one particular weekend, either.

So . . . Mrs. Tweedie had lied. *She* had brought the painters in. *She* had wanted the job done this weekend—and she was paying a lot for it. But why?

"Could it possibly be because Mum and I were going to the city today, to pick up Granny?" Jessie whispered aloud. "Could she possibly have planned the whole thing just so that she could have Blue Moon to herself for once?"

She shook her head violently. No. That was ridiculous. She was letting her imagination run away with her, just as her mother had said. Just as Ms. Stone always said, too.

And it didn't even matter, really. If Mrs. Tweedie *had* made some weird, elaborate plan to give herself a day alone at Blue Moon, her plan had been ruined—first by Jessie's staying home, then by Tasha's coming to stay.

Tasha! Jessie realized that she'd completely forgotten about poor little Tasha.

"Flynn!" she shouted at the top of her voice. "Where are you, Flynn?"

As if in answer, there was a tremendous crash from the shed behind the garage at the side of the house.

Jessie ran to the shed. She could see nothing through the tiny window, but yowls of rage were coming from behind the door, which was bolted shut. Jessie wrestled with the heavy bolt and finally managed to pull it free. She dragged the sagging door open.

Flynn streaked out of the dimness, his orange fur standing on end, his green eyes blazing with fury. The floor of the shed was littered with the smashed remains of the pots he'd pushed off a shelf to attract her attention.

"Flynn! How did you get in there?" Jessie gasped. "Did you follow Mrs. Tweedie in while she was looking for Tasha? Did you get locked in by mistake? Flynn, could you see anything through the window? Do you know where Tasha is?"

Flynn made a furious, huffing sound and raced off through the trees. Jessie's stomach turned over as she saw that he was heading for the secret garden. She ran after him.

The door in the hedge was half open. Flynn ran through the gap. Jessie followed, her heart thudding.

The secret garden was deserted, but something with gauzy pink wings gleamed on the smooth green grass. For a moment Jessie thought it was a real butterfly. Then she realized that it was Tasha's hair clip.

"She's been here, all right," Jessie said, picking up the clip. "But—where did she go after that? She's only little. She wouldn't have been able to walk all the way back up to the street from here and disappear before Mrs. Tweedie started looking for her. Where is she?"

Flynn trilled impatiently. He stared at Jessie fixedly, his tail lashing, as though she was being very stupid.

And Jessie's heart lurched. She remembered Tasha's silver fairy wings. Her grandmother's voice echoed in her mind.

There are Doors to the Realm all over the world, Jessie. But only people who believe in magic can find them.

"Tasha found the Door!" Jessie heard herself saying. "She—she's gone into the Realm! Oh, Flynn!"

Flynn meowed urgently.

Jessie knew what she had to do. She pushed

Tasha's hair clip deep into her pocket. "Open!" she called, and felt herself being swept away.

The next moment, she was blinking in the soft sunlight of the Realm. Quickly she looked around, but there was no sign of Tasha. In fact, there was no one to be seen at all. The pebbly road stretched away to left and right, bare and empty. No white rabbits nibbled the sweet grass beyond. No fairies flitted among the trees.

Jessie called Tasha's name, but there was no answer. Trying not to panic, she realized that by now the little girl might have wandered too far from the Door to hear her. Which way had she gone? Her small feet had left no traces on the pebbles of the road, or on the grass.

"Where are you, Tasha?" Jessie shouted. An aching lump rose in her throat. Tears burned in her eyes.

Stop it! she told herself furiously, fighting back the tears. It's no use standing here blubbering. You've got to get help!

She ran for the palace. By the time she reached it she was gasping for breath and her side was aching, but she didn't stop. She raced down the side of the great golden building till she reached Patrice's door. She pounded on the door with her fists.

For an awful moment she thought there was no one home. Then, with a wave of relief, she heard the sound of hurrying footsteps from inside the little housekeeper's apartment.

"No need to break it down!" shrieked Patrice, throwing the door open with a scowl. "What in the Realm do you think—? Jessie!"

Her frown turned into a look of amazement as Jessie almost fell through the door into her arms.

"Oh—Patrice!" Jessie gasped, and burst into tears.

"Maybelle!" Patrice shrieked. "Giff! Come quickly!"

CHAPTER FIVE

The Rainbow Wand

In moments, Jessie was sitting in Patrice's cozy kitchen and a glass of cool water was being pressed into her hand. Patrice, Maybelle, and Giff huddled around her as, between sobs, she poured out her story.

"Don't cry, Jessie," wailed Giff, whose own eyes had filled with tears at the sight of Jessie's distress. "You don't have to worry about Tasha. All little children are safe in the Realm."

"That's right, dearie," said Patrice gently. "The real dangers—star fairies and Peskies and things like that—are far away from the Doors. Human

49

children who find their way into the Realm are always looked after. They always meet some fairies, or a miniature horse or an elf or someone who'll help them home when it's time."

Maybelle snorted. "Jessie knows that!" she snapped. "That's not the problem. Didn't you hear what she said? That Tweedie woman thinks the little human's lost! She's rushing around trying to find her! She'll have police swarming all over the Blue Moon garden next. It's dangerous, Patrice!"

Giff whimpered, and Patrice's round face clouded. "I hadn't thought of that," she admitted slowly. She turned to Jessie. "Do these police people believe in magic, dearie?" she asked.

Jessie wiped her eyes. "Some of them might," she managed to say. "And, Patrice, if just one gets through the Door, all the others would see! And then—"

"Word would spread," Maybelle said grimly, lashing her tail.

"The newspapers and TV people would hear about it," said Jessie. "In a few days Blue Moon would be crawling with people trying to—"

"No one who means harm can enter the Realm while the magic's strong," Patrice said stoutly.

"Maybe not," growled Maybelle. "But we aren't just talking about people who actually mean harm here, Patrice! We're talking about ordinary, curious humans—thousands of them—flooding into the Realm! Queen Helena would have to lock the Blue Moon Door to stop them. But one by one the other Doors would be found, too. And in the end—Well, in the end, we'd have to cut ourselves off from the human world forever."

She glanced at Jessie. "That's what you're afraid of, Jessie, isn't it?" she asked bluntly.

Jessie nodded, unable to speak.

Patrice pursed her lips. "Well, we'd better find the little girl as quickly as we can, then, and get her home," she said. "The guards can spread the word to everyone within walking distance of the Door: fairies, water sprites, Folk, horses, elves, pixies, unicorns, even the rabbits. Tasha can't have got far. Someone will find her."

She bustled out of the kitchen and disappeared through the door that led into the palace.

"Of course she'll be found in the end, but it'll take time," said Maybelle, tapping a hoof restlessly. "And time is what we don't have if we're going to stop that Tweedie woman from panicking. The girl could be anywhere! If only we knew which way she'd gone."

"The Rainbow Wand could tell us," Giff said suddenly.

Maybelle's hoof stopped tapping. Jessie seized Giff's arm. "What's the Rainbow Wand?" she asked eagerly.

Giff looked startled. "It's . . . um . . . it's a magic wand that finds lost people," he said. "But—"

"Oh, look what you've done, you fool of an elf!" Maybelle shouted, as Jessie jumped to her feet in excitement. "You've got her all fired up now. And you *know* Avron won't let us have the Rainbow Wand!"

"I was just saying—" Giff wailed.

"What's all the shouting about?" scolded Patrice, hurrying back into the room. "Giff! Maybelle! Can't I leave you for five minutes without—"

"Patrice!" exclaimed Jessie. "Giff's just told me

about the Rainbow Wand! Who is Avron? Where can I find him?"

Patrice's plump face went blank. "The—the Rainbow Wand," she said slowly. "Oh, dearie, we can't—"

"I know that for some reason Avron keeps the Rainbow Wand to himself and won't let anyone else use it," Jessie broke in fiercely. "But this time he'll have to change his mind. It's important to the whole Realm! Where does he live? Is it far away?"

"No," said Patrice, smoothing her skirt nervously. "Avron lives in one of the palace towers. But—"

"Then take me to him," Jessie said, almost jumping out of her skin with impatience. "I'll talk to him. I'll *make* him give us the Wand. I'll tell him—tell him Granny wants him to lend it to us. Surely he'd listen then."

Patrice glanced at Maybelle, who had started tapping her hoof again. "We could give it a try, Maybelle," Patrice said. "It can't do any harm to try."

"Oh, no harm at all!" snapped Maybelle. "Getting hit by a thunderbolt or being turned into furry caterpillars will just be a little bit of fun for us, won't it?"

Giff gave a terrified shriek and clapped his hand over his mouth.

Patrice snorted. "Avron had better not try any funny business like that with me," she said crossly. "I've known him since he was in baby robes. I'll take Jessie to the tower by the back way. If you don't want to come with us, then don't!"

Seizing Jessie's arm, she hurried her out of the kitchen and through the door that led to the rest of the palace. "They'll come," she muttered grimly as she and Jessie began to hurry along a deserted corridor.

Jessie looked over her shoulder. Sure enough, far behind her, the door to Patrice's apartment was slowly swinging open again, and Maybelle and Giff were coming out.

"Who *is* Avron, Patrice?" she asked, as the little housekeeper darted up a steep flight of steps. "Why are you all so scared of him?"

"Avron is—or was—the Realm's most brilliant magician." Patrice panted, reaching the top of the steps and beginning to trot along another corridor. "He created hundreds of wonders in his time—the Ribbon Roads, for example."

"And the Rainbow Wand?" Jessie asked quickly.

"Yes," said Patrice. "The Rainbow Wand was his last invention—the one that ruined his life and ended his career." Before Jessie could ask what she meant, she pointed to a door just ahead. "That door leads into Avron's tower," she said. "There's no lock on it—no need for one. Folk know to keep away."

When they reached the door, Patrice leaned against the wall beside it, fanning herself. "I need a minute to catch my breath," she said. "We've got another steep climb ahead of us. Avron's rooms are right at the top of the tower."

Jessie heard the clip-clopping of small hoofs. She turned quickly to see Maybelle and Giff coming down the corridor toward them, looking hot and fearful. "Will Avron really try to hurt us, or—or change us into anything?" she asked, thinking nervously of Maybelle's warning.

Patrice wiped her damp forehead. "He might," she admitted. "I'm hoping he'll listen to what you have to say before he acts, but he's angry and bitter enough to do anything. For twenty-five years the Tower of Avron has been forbidden to everyone—even Queen Helena. Avron speaks to no one."

"But why, Patrice?" Jessie exclaimed. "And why did you say the Rainbow Wand ruined his life?"

"Avron had a child," Patrice said quietly. "Her name was Linnet. Her mother died just after she was born, so she was all Avron had. She was an enchanting little thing—I remember her well, laughing and playing around the palace. Everyone loved her, and as for Avron—well, Linnet was the light of his life. Then—he lost her."

"*Lost* her?" said Jessie. "You mean Linnet died, too?"

"No," said Patrice. "Twenty-five years ago, Linnet just—disappeared."

CHAPTER SIX

The Tower of Avron

As Jessie stared, Patrice bit her lip. "Avron was traveling around the Realm with Linnet," she said. "He was using her to test the Rainbow Wand. He'd ask her to hide from him, in the cleverest places she could think of, and then he'd use the Wand to find her. But one day, while they were in the north . . ."

"One day he *couldn't* find her," Jessie whispered.

Patrice nodded, her round face filled with sorrow. "The Rainbow Wand led Avron to a Door on the Realm's northern border. That Door is hardly ever used because it leads to a busy street in the heart of a human city. Avron realized that Linnet had tried to trick him properly by going into your world. It had never occurred to him that she might do that. She'd never been outside the Realm in her life."

She sighed. "Avron went through the Door himself, of course, but he couldn't find Linnet. Like a lot of magic, the Rainbow Wand doesn't work as strongly in your world as it does in the Realm. It would have sensed Linnet if she'd stayed beside the Door, but she'd wandered away, and of course she'd got lost. She was a bright little girl, but very young—no older than your Tasha."

She shook her head. "Avron searched frantically for months, but it was as if Linnet had disappeared into thin air. At last even he had to admit the search was hopeless. He retreated to his tower and there he's stayed for twenty-five years, alone with his grief. And Linnet has never been seen again."

"That's so—so terrible, Patrice!" Jessie whispered.

Patrice nodded sadly. "Linnet isn't the first of

our children to be lost in your world, dearie, and I don't suppose she'll be the last," she murmured. "If Realm Folk stay too long in your world, their memories fade very quickly. Well, you know that—it's why your grandmother always wears her charm bracelet, to keep her memories of the Realm fresh."

Jessie looked down at her own bracelet. Every one of its charms had been a gift from the Realm. Every one had a story to tell. So far, all the stories had ended happily. But how would this story end?

"It could end with Blue Moon being invaded by thousands of people, and the Realm being cut off from the mortal world forever," she said aloud. "But not if I can find Tasha quickly. Not if I can get the Rainbow Wand."

She looked up and saw Patrice staring at her helplessly. "Come on, Patrice," she said abruptly. "I can't wait a minute longer."

She pulled the tower door open and stepped into the dimness beyond. Before Patrice could follow, the door swung shut again, closing with a loud click.

Startled, Jessie spun around. The doorknob was rattling, twisting uselessly this way and that. "Jessie!" Patrice shrieked, her muffled voice high with panic. "I can't get the door open! Can you do it from your side?"

Jessie tried her best, but the door remained firmly closed. She felt something touch her cheek—something cool, soft, and slightly sticky. She jumped and tried to brush the thing away. It clung to her hand and she saw that it was a thick white thread, like a strand of web spun by a giant spider. Shuddering, Jessie tore her hand free and turned, flattening her back against the door.

Now that her eyes had adjusted to the dimness, she could see that she was in a tall, echoing space with rounded walls. A steep, golden staircase wound up through the center of the space, disappearing into darkness at the top. And hanging all around the staircase, trailing down from the darkness to the floor, were hundreds of the thick white threads.

Jessie shrank back, her heart thudding wildly. Dimly she could hear Patrice, Maybelle, and Giff hitting and kicking the door, but her eyes were fixed on the white threads. They were drifting toward her, swaying closer with every breath she took. Every thread was quivering as if it were alive.

Then she was caught. One moment she was pressed hard against the door. The next moment, the mass of soft, sticky threads had surged against her, wound around her, and jerked her off her feet.

Struggling and screaming, Jessie felt herself being dragged upward. The winding staircase was a golden blur beside her as the threads pulled her up, up through echoing space, like a fish caught in a net. She screwed her eyes tightly shut, her breath was sobbing in her throat. . . .

Then, abruptly, the dizzying upward rush stopped. Jessie felt herself thud onto something firm and warm. She lay, trembling and panting, only dimly aware that the threads that bound her were slipping away.

"Who is this, who has dared to invade my tower?"

The voice was deep and harsh. Jessie opened

her eyes. She was lying on the carpeted floor of a round room lined with books. Light streamed from tall windows, and through the windows she could see the clear blue of the sky.

A tall man in a shining, dark blue robe was looming over her. His proud face, with its pointed black beard and slanting black eyebrows, was deeply marked with lines of bitterness and grief. Jessie knew that this was Avron.

She struggled to sit up. "I am Jessie, the granddaughter of Queen Jessica," she said in a voice that was little more than a squeak. "I have come—"

"I know why you have come," the man said coldly. "The threads that carried you here are my ears as well as my protection. Through them I hear every word that is said outside my walls. You have come to ask me to lend you the Rainbow Wand. And I tell you now that I will not."

"But you must!" Jessie cried, staggering to her feet. "Oh, Avron, you *must*!"

Avron's slanting brows drew together. "It is unwise to use the word 'must' to me, girl," he hissed. "Did you not listen to your friend Patrice? Do you not know my power?"

Jessie felt a thrill of fear. It took all her strength to stop herself from backing away. She swallowed and lifted her chin. "I am sorry," she said, trying to keep her voice from trembling. "It's just—so important that Tasha is found quickly. If she's not—"

Avron's thin lips curved in a bitter smile. "If she is not, the Realm will be overrun by curious humans," he said. "What difference will that make to me? I have already lost everything that gave my life meaning. What do I care what happens now?"

Jessie felt a hot flare of anger. "*You* might not care," she exclaimed passionately. "But everyone else in the Realm does. And my grandmother does. And I do. And Linnet would have cared, too. You know she would!"

As soon as she spoke, she knew she had gone too far, but it was too late to take the hasty words back. Avron's face had twisted with rage. His eyes burned like blue fire. He raised his hand. The floor beneath Jessie's feet trembled. Her skin prickled.

The very air of the tower room seemed to quiver.

Jessie shrank back, covering her eyes, waiting in terror for Avron's fury to burst over her.

But nothing happened. Slowly Jessie's skin stopped prickling, and the room fell silent. Fearfully, she let her hands slide away from her eyes. Avron was standing quite still, his arms hanging loosely by his sides. The anger had drained from his face, leaving a terrible sorrow in its place.

"I'm so sorry," Jessie whispered. "I shouldn't have said that—about Linnet. It was a terrible thing to do."

"No," Avron said in a flat, tired voice. "You said the words that Linnet would have said, if she had been here to speak for herself. My daughter, like her mother before her, was full of life and laughter. She cared for others. She would have begged me to lend the Rainbow Wand, to save the Realm. And so . . . for her sake . . . I shall."

The relief was so great that Jessie felt weak at the knees. She clasped her hands to stop them from trembling.

Avron went to a carved wooden chest that stood beneath one of the windows. He lifted the lid of the chest and took something out. When he turned back to Jessie he was holding a plain, polished silver rod.

"This is the Rainbow Wand," he said curtly. "It is tuned to find Linnet, and always will be, while I live, but the tuning may be changed for a short time. To do this I need an object belonging to the Lost One."

"An object . . . ?" For an instant Jessie's heart seemed to stand still. Then she remembered. She pulled the butterfly hair clip from her pocket and held it out.

Avron took the clip and touched it to the tip of the Rainbow Wand, muttering some words that Jessie couldn't hear. The tip of the wand lit with a strange blue glow.

Avron handed the hair clip back to Jessie, then placed the glowing wand in her eager hands. As she began to gasp her thanks, he shook his head. "Do not thank me yet," he said gravely. "You must beware. The Rainbow Wand is very powerful, and it was never truly finished. I put it aside when Linnet was lost."

He frowned. "Had I continued with my work, the wand would have been made safe. As it is, it could be dangerous. You must follow my instructions exactly, or you may do more harm with it than good. Do you understand?"

"Yes," Jessie said breathlessly. "Yes, Avron. Just tell me what to do."

the snairies

Not long afterward, Jessie, Patrice, Maybelle, and Giff were running down the front steps of the Palace.

"Oh, Jessie, I still can't believe you're safe!" Patrice panted. "When I couldn't open that door I was just so—"

"Stop going on and on about it, Patrice," Maybelle interrupted impatiently. "Let's hear what Avron said about the Rainbow Wand."

"He said that the wand will change color to show us which way we have to go to find Tasha," Jessie said. "If the tip is blue or green—what

Avron called *cold* colors—it means we're going the wrong way. But if the tip turns from yellow to orange to red—*hot* colors—it's telling us that we're going the *right* way."

"So that's why we came out this way, Jessie," Giff said excitedly as they reached the bottom of the steps. "Because while you were inside, the wand went yellow when you pointed it toward the front of the palace. Oh, that's so clever! Do the colors *feel* hot and cold?" He stretched out a finger to touch the glowing tip of the wand.

With a cry of alarm, Jessie jerked it out of his reach. "No, Giff!" She gasped. "It's dangerous for the wand to touch anyone except the Lost One it's tuned to find. That's another thing Avron told me. He's not sure what would happen if the wand touched someone else, but he thinks there'd be some sort of explosion, at least."

Giff snatched his finger back, looking horrified.

"And the brighter the wand is, the more dangerous it is, I suppose," Patrice asked nervously. "You'll be very careful, won't you, Jessie?"

Jessie nodded. "Don't worry, Patrice," she

said. "As soon as I've got Tasha home, I just have to say, 'The Lost One is found,' and the spell will be broken. The wand will change back to normal, and be safe again."

"Let's get on with it, then!" Maybelle snorted. "The sooner we're rid of the thing, the better!"

Jessie held the Rainbow Wand out in front of her and swept it slowly from side to side. The moment it pointed toward the grove of pale-leaved trees that stood at the edge of the grass, the yellow tip brightened and deepened to gold.

"That way!" Maybelle exclaimed in excitement, and Jessie ran, with the Rainbow Wand held high and her friends close behind her.

They threaded their way through the trees, keeping their eyes on the glowing tip of the wand. Jessie waved the wand this way and that as she walked, always moving in the direction that made the golden glow burn brightest.

Soon they were deep inside the grove. The ground was covered in a thick carpet of dead leaves, and their feet made a soft rustling sound as they walked. There was no other noise except the whispering of the trees.

Then Jessie saw something strange hanging from the lowest branch of a tree not far ahead. It was a large, round ball that seemed to be made of twigs and leaves woven together.

She was just about to ask what it was when she heard Patrice, Maybelle, and Giff exclaim in dismay.

"What's the matter?" Jessie whispered.

"There's a snairie nest ahead," Maybelle muttered in her ear. "See that big round thing hanging in the tree? By the look of it, the snairies aren't at home, so we'd better be careful. They like hiding under dead leaves, you know, the silly things."

"Snairies?" asked Jessie, her eyes still fixed on the tip of the Rainbow Wand. "What are—?"

And at that very moment, she trod on something round and bouncy. The thing squeaked loudly, and Jessie jumped backward with a cry of shock.

A small, round creature erupted from the forest floor in a shower of dead leaves, squeaking indignantly. The creature's body was not much bigger than a tennis ball. It had big blue eyes and very large bright pink feet. Otherwise, it was completely covered in long, silky brown hair.

"Oh, I'm really sorry!" Jessie exclaimed. "I didn't mean to tread on you."

Still squeaking, the little creature began bouncing up and down like a hairy ball with feet. Then, suddenly, the forest floor was dotted with what looked like tiny explosions of dead leaves. Other snairies were popping up everywhere, their blue eyes wide and startled.

Jessie took another step backward. "Will they hurt us?" she whispered.

"Of course not," snorted Maybelle, pawing the ground. "They'll only waste our time. Snairies are very good at that, and they enjoy it, too."

"Well, they haven't got anything else to do, have they?" Patrice said distractedly. "Has anyone got any peppermints?"

"I've got two," Giff squeaked. "I was saving them for—"

"Give them to me, Giff," ordered Patrice, holding out her hand.

"But I was saving them for—" Giff began.

"Give her the peppermints!" shouted Maybelle. "This is an emergency!"

Sulkily, Giff took two rather worn-looking peppermints from under his cap, and gave them to Patrice. Patrice put them onto the palm of her hand and held them out to the snairie Jessie had trodden on.

"Treats!" she cooed in a singsong voice. "Treats, to say sorry for the hurt."

The snairie glanced around at its friends. "Treats," it said longingly.

"A riddle!" chorused the other snairies, bouncing up and down and slapping the dead leaves with their big pink feet. "A riddle, *then* treats, when we get the answer!"

"Oh, no," Giff groaned.

Maybelle frowned, lashing her tail furiously. "Listen, snairies!" she snapped. "We're on important business. We haven't got time to stand around asking you riddles!"

The snairies looked at one another. Then, as if obeying some secret signal, they all dived back under the leaves. The leaves heaved and rustled, then grew silent, but Jessie could feel several small, round bodies pressing against the toes of her shoes.

"Look what you've done, Maybelle!" Patrice said crossly. "Now they'll keep rolling under our feet so we tread on them with every step we take. You know how they are."

"Well, let's just tread on them, then," bellowed Maybelle, in a temper. "I don't care if every one of the stupid, useless things is squashed flat!"

"Oh, don't say that!" cried Jessie in distress. "We mustn't hurt them!"

Patrice sighed. "We'll have to ask them a riddle," she said. "It's the only way."

"I know lots of riddles," Jessie said eagerly. "What about — ?"

"Be careful, Jessie!" Giff whimpered, shuffling his feet nervously. "They're listening!"

"It has to be a really, really easy riddle, dearie," Patrice explained in a low voice as Jessie glanced at Giff in surprise. "If the snairies can't think of an answer, they'll get upset."

"Then they'll roll under our feet even more," moaned Giff. "We'll be stuck here for ages. That happened to my mother once."

"What did she ask them?" Jessie whispered.

"She couldn't think of anything," Giff whispered back. "So the snairies all crowded around her feet and wouldn't move. She didn't want to tread on them, so she had to sleep the night in the forest, standing up!"

Maybelle snorted in disgust.

"Jessie!" hissed Patrice. "Look at the wand!"

Jessie felt a thrill of fear as she saw that the golden tip of the Rainbow Wand was fading to yellow. She thought frantically.

"Give me the peppermints, Patrice," she said at last. When she had the peppermints in her hand she held them out and cleared her throat. "All right, snairies!" she called. "Here's a riddle for you!"

Dead leaves flew into the air as the snairies popped their heads up again. "Now, listen carefully," Jessie said. "What has a name beginning with S, has two blue eyes and two pink feet, is covered in brown hair, has a round nest, hides under dead leaves, and loves to answer riddles?"

The snairies stood motionless, thinking hard.

"Not a brain in their heads," muttered Maybelle, ignoring Patrice's frantic shushing sounds.

The snairies began whispering together. They seemed to be having an argument.

"How could they *possibly* not know the answer?" Jessie whispered in despair.

"You don't know snairies," Maybelle said darkly.

But just then, the snairie Jessie had trodden on looked up. "Is . . . is the answer, 'a snairie'?" it said hesitantly.

"Yes!" Jessie exclaimed.

All the snairies began bouncing up and down. "We were right! We were right!" they squeaked together. "Treats!" And without any warning, they all leaped wildly at the peppermints in Jessie's outstretched hand.

Taken by surprise, Jessie staggered backward, losing her balance. The Rainbow Wand twisted in her hand. The snairies crashed into it headlong. There was a blinding flash and a sharp, cracking sound.

Jessie screamed in fright. For a moment she could see nothing but stars, and when at last her eyes cleared, the forest floor was deserted. The snairies had completely disappeared. "Oh, no!" she cried in horror.

"It's all right!" Giff squealed. "Look!" He pointed at the snairie nest, which was now studded all over with pairs of bright pink feet, as if the snairies had dived in headfirst.

"The wand sent them home!" exclaimed Patrice. "Oh, quickly, let's get out of here before they come out again!"

CHAPTER EIGHT

THE LOST ONE

As Jessie led the way past the snairie nest, one of the pairs of feet disappeared inside, and a hairy face with two bright blue eyes peeped out. Jessie thought she recognized the snairie she'd trodden on, and her stomach lurched.

"Hello," mumbled the snairie. "Who are you?"

"Oh, no one special," Patrice said quickly. "Don't let us disturb you."

The snairie nodded sleepily. It ducked back into the nest again, and the next moment the four friends were staring at the soles of its feet once more, and gentle snores were filling the air.

"They've forgotten us already!" called Jessie as she and the others ran on. "Do you think the Rainbow Wand made them lose their memories?"

"It might have." Patrice puffed. "It must have given them an awful shock when it flashed and blew them home like that. Lucky it was only yellow at the time. Otherwise—"

She broke off as Jessie gave a joyous cry and held the wand high. The tip was rapidly brightening, changing from yellow to gold to orange. "Tasha must be very near!" Jessie shouted. "Come on!"

The Rainbow Wand led Jessie, Patrice, Maybelle, and Giff out of the grove of pale-leafed trees, and into a thick mass of berry bushes. It was shining more brightly every moment, but there was still no sign of Tasha.

"Where are we?" Jessie shouted over her shoulder.

There was no answer. Surprised, she slowed down and looked back. All her friends were smiling.

"We should have known," Maybelle said gruffly.

"Of *course*!" Patrice sighed.

"They miss Queen Helena," Giff said. "You can't really blame them."

"What are you talking about?" Jessie demanded. "What do you—?"

Then she pushed through the last of the berry bushes. And, dazzled by the flaming red light of the Rainbow Wand, she blinked at what was ahead.

It was a field of giant flowers—flowers of every kind, some as tall as small trees, bending and swaying in the soft Realm breeze.

Filled with wonder, Jessie moved forward. Rich brown earth crumbled beneath her feet. Slender green stems and leaves swayed all around her. Soft colors blended above her head. Sweet perfumes scented the air, which was filled with soft, faint music as if the flowers themselves were singing.

The Rainbow Wand was brightening every moment. Jessie told herself she should be calling Tasha's name, but somehow she couldn't bear to break into the sound of the flowers' song. Then she saw a small green space ahead—a round clearing in the middle of the flower field. Jessie began to move faster, but as she reached the clearing's edge, she stopped, staring.

A little blue rabbit was joyfully hopping around the clearing, pausing now and then to nibble the soft green grass. High above the rabbit's head, dancing in a ring with glorious flowers nodding all around them were Daisy, Violet, Daffodil, Bluebell, and Rose. And in the middle of their circle, eyes sparkling, silver wings fluttering and alive, danced Tasha.

"Jessie!" squeaked Daffodil, seeing Jessie and turning an excited somersault in the air. "You've come back after all! Oh, what a beautiful wand! See how brightly it shines!"

The Rainbow Wand was blazing. Its tip was a glittering scarlet star. Tasha looked down, and her eyes widened.

"Did you fairies bring this little girl into the Realm?" said Patrice sternly. "How could you! You *know* it's against the rules."

"We didn't bring her!" cried Daffodil indignantly. "She came in all by herself!"

Tasha nodded proudly. "I went into your special

garden and I said, 'Open,' and my hair blew around," she said to Jessie. "And then I was in fairyland."

"We met Tasha on the pebbly road," Rose broke in, holding out her full pink skirts and twirling around. "She was all alone except for Bunny. And when we asked her if she'd dance with us, she said yes! She said she'd *love* to dance with us. And she had her own wings and everything."

"So we brought her to the Forest of Flowers with us," Violet put in shyly.

"That was a good idea, Jessie, wasn't it?" shouted Daffodil. "Because Tasha likes flowers. And Bunny likes them, too."

Tasha's face was shining. Jessie couldn't bring herself to do anything more than smile and nod.

"It was a lovely idea," she said gently. "But Tasha shouldn't have left Blue Moon without asking her mother. We've been very worried, and we've been looking for her everywhere. Anyway, now it's time for her to come home."

"Oh, no!" wailed the fairies. "Not yet!"

Jessie had expected Tasha to argue, too, but the little girl just nodded sadly. "I have to go now," she told the flower fairies. "Jessie says."

Silver wings fluttering, she let herself drift slowly to the ground. "Come on, Bunny," she said. The little blue rabbit jumped into her arms, and she began skipping toward Jessie through the flowers.

"Don't come too near the wand, fairies," Jessie warned as the fairies began to follow. "It might hurt you."

She saw how disappointed they looked and thought quickly. "Can you fly in front of us, though?" she added. "Can you lead us back to the Door by the quickest way?"

"*I* know the quickest way," said Maybelle. "Why in the Realm—?" Patrice nudged her sharply and she fell silent.

Very pleased to have an important job to do, Daisy, Buttercup, Rose, Violet, and Bluebell flew over to a stem of pink-spotted bells, and perched there, waiting.

Tasha reached Jessie's side and took her hand.

Jessie's whole arm tingled, and the Rainbow Wand flamed like a fiery star.

"That thing's looking dangerous," Maybelle muttered nervously. "Say the words to break the spell, Jessie."

"Not till Tasha's safely home," Jessie said. "I'm not taking any risks." She smiled at Tasha. "Look what I found," she said, digging into her pocket and bringing out the butterfly hair clip. Tasha beamed as the butterfly was clipped to her hair once more.

"This way!" squeaked Daffodil, beckoning importantly. "This way!"

Following the fairies, Jessie began to lead Tasha through the flowers, with Patrice, Giff, and Maybelle following in single file behind.

"Are you a fairy princess, Jessie?" Tasha asked breathlessly.

"She certainly is, dearie," said Patrice warmly, just as Jessie was about to deny that she was any such thing.

"I knew she was," said Tasha. "She has a fairy princess wand." She yawned and cuddled Bunny closer to her chest. She was clearly very sleepy, but she trotted beside Jessie without complaint as the fairies led them out of the Forest of Flowers, through a group of trees with silver bark, and on to the pebbly road.

When at last the Door came into view, even Jessie was feeling tired. It seemed to her that she'd been in the Realm for ages, though the sun was still high in the sky, so she knew it hadn't been so very long at all.

"With a bit of luck, Mrs. Tweedie will still be out searching the streets," she whispered to Patrice, Maybelle, and Giff. "I might be able to get Tasha into the house before she gets back."

"The Tweedie woman won't be satisfied with that," Maybelle muttered. "She'll want to know where the child has been. She'll ask her all sorts of questions."

"I've thought of that," Jessie said. "If I can get Tasha back to the house, I'll put her on my bed to lie down. She's really tired—I'm sure she'll go straight to sleep. Then I'll tell Mrs. Tweedie she was there all the time."

"You might get away with it," Patrice said doubtfully. "We'll keep our fingers crossed."

"And our toes," said Giff.

The flower fairies hovered in front of the Door, their wings bright in the sunlight. "We'll come with you, Jessie," said Daffodil brightly. "Then we can look for sweetie-pies again."

"If greedy Emerald hasn't found them all," said Rose, licking her lips.

"No, no," Jessie said firmly. "Tasha and I have to go alone this time. You stay where you are. And if Emerald's in the secret garden, I'll send her home, too."

Holding the Rainbow Wand carefully to one side, she bent and picked up Tasha. "Hold tight, Tasha," she said softly.

The little girl waved to the fairies, Patrice, Maybelle, and Giff. Then she put her arm around Jessie's neck. Jessie turned and faced the door.

"Open!" she said. Everything grew dark. Her hair began to blow around her head. The cool wind tingled on her face. She could faintly hear the sounds of her friends calling good-bye and wishing her luck. She could feel Tasha clinging to her.

And then there was grass beneath her feet, and she could hear Flynn yowling somewhere nearby. Her arm was aching with Tasha's weight. She opened her eyes, and at once they began to water in the sunlight. Sighing with relief, she dropped the Rainbow Wand, then bent and let Tasha slide to the ground.

"We're back, Bunny," she heard the little girl yawn. "We're back from the Realm."

"So you are, you clever girl!" cooed a fake-sweet voice. "And now you can tell me all about it, can't you?"

Jessie jerked upright, spun around, and found herself looking straight into the cold, triumphant eyes of Mrs. Tweedie.

CHAPTER NINE

The Trap

"Don't bother trying to make up a story to explain this, Jessie," said Mrs. Tweedie as Jessie gaped at her, speechless with shock. "I saw Tasha disappear through the Door, I saw you go after her, and just now I saw you both come back. I saw it with my own eyes—just as I'd planned."

She waited, a smile curving her thin lips, while slowly Jessie made sense of what she'd said, and Flynn yowled on the other side of the door in the hedge.

"You knew where Tasha was all the time," Jessie whispered. "That note you left for me was a

95

lie. You sent Tasha to the Realm, and then you tricked me into going after her."

"Quite. And I watched it all from the top of a ladder on the other side of the hedge," Mrs. Tweedie said, her smile broadening. "You didn't notice me—even that cat didn't see me till I came down. Then it attacked me, the vicious brute!"

She looked down at her hands, which were covered in deep scarlet scratches, then glanced at the door in the hedge, as if to make sure that Flynn was still safely locked outside.

"I admit I was very annoyed when you insisted on staying home today, Jessie," she went on. "I'd gone to a lot of trouble to get Blue Moon to myself, and arrange to babysit Tasha on the same day. Then I realized that you could make my plan even better. So I set my little trap, and you fell into it."

Jessie wet her lips. "No one will believe you if you tell," she said. "They'll say you were seeing things."

"I'm not Mr. Bins, Jessie," said Mrs. Tweedie softly. "I'm famous for investigating mysteries like this. Well, you should know. You're reading one of my books, after all."

She raised an eyebrow, waiting for Jessie to realize what she meant. And slowly, with cold, prickling horror, Jessie did.

"You're L. T. Bowers." Jessie gasped.

"That's right," the woman said, her voice hardening. "Louise Tweedie Bowers. When the Bins family moved into my apartment building, it was the stroke of luck I'd been waiting for all my writing life. I'd always been interested in Robert Belairs. Those fairy paintings of his are so detailed—so *real*! Then I heard what the Bins family had to say, and the rest is history—or will be."

She pointed to a place near the top of the hedge. Something glinted there: the lens of her video camera, wedged between dense leaves.

"Everything that has happened here today has been recorded," she said, eyeing Jessie's shocked face with satisfaction. "And I've taken hundreds of still photographs over the past few months, too, of course. My readers like pictures."

Jessie felt sick. "You planned it all," she said in a low voice. "You came here to spy on us. You—"

"I've also got sound recordings," Mrs. Tweedie cut in. "Lately I've had plenty of chances to plant a recording device in here for a day or two. That's how I knew to tell Tasha that the magic word was 'Open.'"

Jessie looked quickly over her shoulder. Tasha had curled up on the grass and gone peacefully to sleep with her blue rabbit in her arms. Beside her lay the butterfly hair clip, which had again fallen from her tangled curls.

"Sweet!" purred Mrs. Tweedie. "Oh, she'll be wonderful on television."

"You can't write about this, Mrs. Tweedie," Jessie said, trying to control the trembling in her voice. "You'll destroy Blue Moon. You'll threaten the Realm itself. You can't—"

Mrs. Tweedie laughed. "If you think that I left my lovely, convenient apartment and camped for months in that dreadful house next door for fun, you're wrong," she said. "Today is my last day here, and I couldn't be happier. I've already returned the car to the rental company, and sent all my things back to the city—well, except for the evidence, of course. I wouldn't let that out of my sight." She patted the little overnight bag at her feet and sighed with pleasure.

"This will be the biggest story of my life," she went on smugly. "After the first few newspaper stories and TV interviews, publishers will be wild to get the book. I'll be able to name my own price. Oh, the timing is perfect! People who'd never heard of Robert Belairs or Blue Moon know all about them now, because of the exhibition."

She glanced at her watch. "Actually, some people from one of the TV stations should be here any minute," she added casually. "A news story tonight will get the ball rolling."

Jessie clenched her fists. "I'll tell them that nothing you say is true," she said in a low voice. "I'll tell them that you faked the video, and the pictures, and everything."

"Say what you like," drawled Mrs. Tweedie. "Tasha is a very truthful little girl. *She* won't tell fibs. It was a very good idea to use her for my little experiment."

"You only used Tasha because you couldn't get into the Realm yourself," Jessie burst out. "You probably tried over and over again, but you couldn't do it. I suppose you think it's because you're a grown-up, but it's not! It's because you're mean and selfish and horrible, and the Realm won't have you!"

Anger flashed in Mrs. Tweedie's eyes. "Thank you for that information," she sneered. "And now, here's something for you to think about!"

She turned around, felt under a rosemary bush, and pulled out a small green cage. Jessie went cold as she saw, crouching behind the narrow bars, a tiny, terrified figure with soft green wings: the rainbow fairy Emerald.

Jessie jumped forward, but Mrs. Tweedie swung the cage out of her reach. There was a rattling sound and a tiny striped sweet rolled through the bars and fell onto the grass.

In a flash, Jessie saw what she should have realized long ago. It was Mrs. Tweedie who had been leaving treats for the fairies in the secret garden. She'd been doing it for weeks, ever since Granny went away. And this morning she'd laid her trap, knowing that she was sure to catch at least one fairy by the end of the day.

"I don't think there'll be any risk of people thinking I'm a fake when they see this, do you?" Mrs. Tweedie said softly.

"Hello?" a crisp female voice called from behind the door in the hedge. "Ms. Bowers?"

"Ye-es!" caroled Mrs. Tweedie, pushing Jessie away and returning the cage to its hiding place.

The door opened and Flynn streaked in, nearly tripping up the smartly dressed young woman and the tall, bearded man standing outside. Mrs. Tweedie shrank back in alarm, but Flynn just leaped under a rosemary bush and crouched there in sullen silence.

"Ms. Bowers? I'm Sharon Bliss. We spoke on the phone," the young woman said, moving forward and holding out her hand to Mrs. Tweedie.

"Good to meet you," said Mrs. Tweedie, shaking hands. She smiled at the bearded man, who was carrying a TV camera.

"Kel Pike," he said with a casual nod. He lifted the camera onto his shoulder. "Where's this fairy, then?" he asked. He sounded as if he was trying not to laugh. Sharon glanced at him warningly.

"Louise, have you lost your mind?" snapped a voice.

Everyone jumped and turned. Ms. Stone was

standing in the doorway, her face rigid with anger. "I was outside in my car, waiting to speak to Jessica's mother when she got home, when these people arrived," she said icily. "They told me — they told me that they'd come to interview a woman who claimed to have caught a — a *fairy*."

"That's right," said Mrs. Tweedie calmly.

"Louise!" Ms. Stone snapped. "It's bad enough making a fool of yourself, but how *could* you drag Jessica into this? The child's damaged enough as it is. That grandmother of hers —" She broke off and swung around to Sharon Bliss. "This is just a stupid publicity stunt for the Belairs exhibition; can't you see that?" she exclaimed. "How *can* you go along with it?"

Sharon shrugged. "People like fun stories like this on a Sunday night," she said. "The boss says that L. T. Bowers is always good for a laugh."

"L. T. Bowers?" hissed Ms. Stone, staring at her. "But —"

"I think it's time to put an end to all this," Mrs. Tweedie said coldly. She lifted the cage from behind her and held it up with a small, triumphant smile.

Everyone stared. Gauzy wings glimmered behind bars as the cage swung in Mrs. Tweedie's hand.

There was a short, deadly silence.

"We can't do anything with this, Sharon," said Kel Pike at last. "No way. She didn't even try to give it a face, or legs, or anything."

Mrs. Tweedie looked into the cage, and her eyes bulged. The cage tilted, the door swung open, and Tasha's butterfly hair clip slid out and dropped softly to the ground.

Tears of relief welled up in Jessie's eyes. She clapped her hands over her mouth to hold back hysterical laughter. She heard a soft trill behind her and swung around. Flynn was sitting there, calmly washing his paws, to which fragments of earth still clung. He met her eyes and blinked.

Mrs. Tweedie pointed at him, beside herself with rage. "It was that cat!" she shrieked. "The cat crept around behind the bushes! He let the fairy out, and put this thing in its place!" She kicked at the butterfly hair clip, and missed.

"The cat," drawled Kel Pike. "Sure." He looked

at Sharon Bliss, and jerked his head toward the door.

"Yes. Well. We'll be off, then," Sharon said in a high voice. "Thanks very much."

The two of them almost ran through the door and out into the garden beyond. With a final, appalled glance at Mrs. Tweedie, Ms. Stone stalked after them, obviously intending to make sure they actually left.

"Stop grinning, you stupid girl!" Mrs. Tweedie snarled at Jessie. "This doesn't make a scrap of difference! I still have the pictures and the tapes. The whole world's going to know about you and this place. I said, *Get that smile off your face!*"

Wild with fury, she hurled the empty cage at Jessie. Flynn sprang at her like an orange fury.

"Get away from me, you brute!" the woman shrieked. She tore the biting, scratching cat away from her and threw him aside. Flynn landed lightly and spun around, ready to attack again.

Mrs. Tweedie looked around for a weapon. Her eyes fell on the Rainbow Wand lying on the grass where Jessie had dropped it. Teeth bared, she leaped for it.

"No!" Jessie screamed. "No—"

Mrs. Tweedie grabbed the wand with both hands. Instantly it was as if the secret garden had been struck by scarlet lightning. There was an ear-splitting crack. . . .

And when Jessie was able to look again, the grass was littered with charred fragments of leather and melted plastic, Flynn was peacefully washing his paws once more, and Mrs. Tweedie had gone.

surprises

Trembling with shock, Jessie crawled to the Rainbow Wand and took it in her hand. "The Lost One is found," she mumbled. At once the wand faded, becoming a plain silver rod once more.

"Something went bang, Jessie."

Jessie turned around. Tasha was sitting up, rubbing her eyes. "Never mind," Jessie said hurriedly. She picked up the butterfly hair clip from the grass, and took it to the little girl. "You lost this again," she said, clipping the butterfly to the dark curls.

"Well, hello, you two," said a bright voice from the door.

"Mummy!" squealed Tasha. She scrambled up and ran to the smiling woman, who crouched to hug her.

"You must be Jessie," the woman said, smiling at Jessie over her daughter's head. "I'm Alice, Tasha's mum. Thank you so much for looking after her today. Where's Mrs. Tweedie?"

"I'm—I'm not sure," Jessie stammered, getting unsteadily to her feet. "She . . . um . . . went somewhere."

"Oh," Alice said. "Well, could you thank her very much for me? I'd like to get Tasha home. I think a storm might be coming. I heard thunder a moment ago." She stood up with Tasha in her arms. "Home we go, sweetie," she said as Tasha snuggled into her shoulder. "Oh, you're a tired girl, aren't you?"

Tasha nodded sleepily. "I went to sleep on the grass," she said. "Mum? I went to fairyland. I danced with flower fairies. And I met an elf, and a little white horse that talked. And Jessie was a fairy princess with a magic wand."

"Is that so?" her mother said, glancing at Jessie with a puzzled smile. Jessie held her breath.

"Yes," Tasha said. "And Mum? Bunny came alive." She sighed happily, and yawned. "I like sleeping on grass," she added, closing her eyes. "That was the bestest dream I ever had."

Alice kissed the top of her head, waved good-bye to Jessie, and hurried away through the trees. Flynn went with her, but Jessie stayed at the doorway of the secret garden. Her legs were trembling so much that she wasn't sure they would carry her. She stood motionless, staring at nothing.

Tasha thought that the Realm had been a dream, a wonderful dream. Jessie felt as if she were living in a dream right now. Her mind was numb. Blue Moon was safe. The Realm was safe. But . . . Mrs. Tweedie. What had the Rainbow Wand done to Mrs. Tweedie?

Suddenly she realized that something was moving among the trees. She blinked, and as her eyes came back into focus her heart leaped. Her grandmother was hurrying toward the secret garden, still dressed in the blue skirt and loose, flowered jacket she wore for traveling. Flynn was trotting by Granny's side, his tail held high.

Neither of them seemed to be aware that Ms. Stone was following them. Jessie groaned aloud. Oh, why won't Stoneface leave me alone? she thought desperately. I've got to talk to Granny by herself. I've just got to!

"Jessie, are you all right?" Granny exclaimed, reaching Jessie and hugging her tightly. "When Flynn told me I . . . Oh, Jessie, I can't believe I left you to face this alone! I'm so sorry!"

"I should think so!" snapped Ms. Stone, striding up behind her, breathing hard. "You should be ashamed of yourself, Mrs. Belairs—involving your granddaughter in a crude publicity stunt. And as for that poor, silly Louise Tweedie—"

Granny turned around. "I don't think we've met," she said mildly, looking up into Ms. Stone's frozen face. Then she stiffened. "Oh, you poor child," she murmured, in quite a different voice. And to Jessie's astonishment, she reached out and took Ms. Stone's hands in both her own.

Ugly patches of crimson appeared on Ms. Stone's cheeks and neck. A strange, almost frightened, expression sprang into her eyes. "Let me go!" she gasped, trying to wrench her hands free.

Granny held on. It was as if, suddenly, she had twice her usual strength. Jessie's skin prickled. "Granny," she whispered urgently. "It's Ms. Stone—you know—my schoolteacher!"

Granny didn't answer. Her eyes were fixed on Ms. Stone's. "Don't be afraid, my dear," she said softly, backing through the secret garden doorway and pulling the terrified-looking woman with her. "All will be well. Come with me, now. Come on."

Amazed and fearful, Jessie stumbled out of the way as slowly but surely her grandmother drew Ms. Stone into the center of the secret garden.

And, without warning, the Rainbow Wand blazed with radiant light. Jessie screamed as sparks flew from the burning star at its tip, showering the soft green grass, the fragrant rosemary, like scarlet rain.

What could this mean? Why was the wand acting as if . . . as if . . . ?

*It is tuned to find Linnet, and always will be, while I
live . . .*

"It can't be!" Jessie whispered as Avron's voice
echoed in her mind. She turned and stared at Ms.
Stone, who was cowering away from the blinding
glare. She felt her grandmother push Ms. Stone's
hand into hers. "Open!" Granny called in a thun-
derous voice.

Jessie's hair began to fly around her head. Ms.
Stone whimpered beside her. As darkness closed
in, her grandmother's voice rang in her ears.

"Lyn Stone is a Lost One, Jessie!" Granny
called. "That wand knows it—and I knew it the
minute I set eyes on her! Don't you see? That's
why she's hated magic for so long. It's in her
blood! It made her a stranger in this world, but
she didn't know why, so she's been afraid of it for
most of her life. Take her home, Jessie! Take the
poor child home!"

An hour later, Jessie came back to Blue Moon.
She found her mother and grandmother in the
kitchen drinking tea and eating pastries they'd

bought on their way home from the airport.

"I'm so glad you decided to go out after all, Jess," Rosemary said when the greetings were over and Jessie had joined them at the table. "Really, you were quite right about Louise Tweedie. She's a very peculiar woman. Do you know, she's just packed up and left?"

"Really?" Jessie said weakly.

"Yes!" Rosemary exclaimed. "And, what's more, she seems to have been burning rubbish in the garden. There are little bits of melted plastic and metal and paper all over the grass. I'll really give her a piece of my mind when she turns up again!"

Jessie sank her teeth into an apricot pastry. "I don't think she will," she said with her mouth full. "I think she's gone home—back where she came from—and that she's forgotten all about us."

Rosemary laughed. "I wish!" she said.

Jessie smiled. She knew she was right. After all, as Patrice had reminded her just half an hour ago, that's what had happened to the snairies when *they* touched the Rainbow Wand.

"Oh," said Granny, stretching out her legs, comfortable in old slacks once more. "It's wonderful to be back at Blue Moon,"

"It certainly is," Rosemary agreed. "One day in the city was enough for me." She took a deep breath and looked at Jessie, who had just taken another big bite of her pastry.

"Today I spoke to our lawyer, and also to the real estate agent who manages the renting of our old house, Jess," she said. "The young couple who rent the house have wanted to buy it for ages, you know. They're offering a good price, they're nice people, and I'm tired of having all that money tied up in a house we'll never live in again. So finally I've told the agent that, yes, we'll sell. Why not? Our home is here now."

Jessie nearly choked on her pastry. "Mum!" she spluttered. "You mean . . . *that's* why you went to the city so early?"

"Well, yes," said Rosemary, smiling. "I didn't tell you before because I wanted to make sure it was really going to happen."

"Well, this *is* exciting!" Granny said, her eyes

twinkling. "What made you decide at last, my darling?"

Rosemary shrugged. "Oh, I don't know," she said, not looking at Jessie. "Yesterday, I talked to someone who—who was obviously very bitter and very unhappy, but still wanted everyone else to live their lives the way she did. I was very sad for her. She didn't seem to understand how important it is to love what you do—whatever it is, and whatever form it takes."

She put down her cup and sighed. "Talking to her made me realize that you should treasure happiness and trust it," she said. "And home— Well, home is where the heart is, as they say." She wiped a trace of dampness from her eyes and laughed self-consciously.

Jessie flung her arms around her mother's neck and hugged her. Her mind was full of pictures. She remembered Ms. Stone—Linnet of the Realm now—her shining hair streaming down her back, her eyes glowing, her face alive with happiness. She thought of stern Avron weeping with joy because his child had been found. She thought of

Patrice, Giff, Maybelle, and all the Folk celebrating the return of their Lost One, and the golden palace ringing with their songs of joy.

"You're so right, Mum!" she said. "You're so really, really right!"

Rosemary laughed again. "I knew you'd be pleased," she said. Then she looked carefully at the charm bracelet on Jessie's wrist. "Oh, Jessie, you've got a new charm!" she exclaimed. "A little gold crown. Isn't that sweet? Where did it come from?"

"Jessie earned it, I'd say," Granny said, beaming. "I'd say that someone decided that every true, brave princess should have a crown to call her own. Isn't that so, Jessie?"

And Jessie, thinking of Avron's words as he fastened the tiny crown in place, blushed, and nodded.

"May you always feel for others, as you do now," Avron had said, with a deep bow. "May you always remember the importance of laughter. And may there always be magic in your heart. Then, Princess Jessie of the Realm, you will indeed live happily ever after."

EMILY RODDA

has written many books for children, including the Deltora Quest and Rowan of Rin books. She has won the Children's Book Council of Australia Book of the Year Award an unprecedented five times, and her books have been translated into twenty-four languages and published in thirty countries. A former editor, Ms. Rodda has also written adult mysteries under the name Jennifer Rowe. She lives in Australia. You can visit her online at www.emilyrodda.com.